Vera B. Williams

CHERRIES AND CHERRY PITS

Greenwillow Books, New York

Cherries and Cherry Pits
Copyright © 1986 by Vera B. Williams
All rights reserved.
Printed in Hong Kong by South China Printing Company (1988) Ltd.
www.harperchildrens.com
First Edition 12 11 10 9 8 7

The full-color artwork was prepared as watercolor paintings and,
for the pictures of Bidemmi, as felt-tipped pen drawings.
The typeface is Benguiat Gothic Medium.

Library of Congress Cataloging-in-Publication Data

Williams, Vera B.
Cherries and cherry pits.
"Greenwillow Books."
Summary: Bidemmi draws pictures and tells stories.
[1. Cherry—Fiction] I. Title.
PZ7.W6685Ci 1986   [E]   85-17156
ISBN 0-688-05145-6 (trade)
ISBN 0-688-05146-4 (lib. bdg.)
ISBN 0-688-10478-9 (pbk.)

Dear Papa
I still remember how you
told me all those stories
and how you saved the
drawings I made and how
you listened to the stories
I told you.
love
Vera

TO THE MEMORY OF ALBERT S. BAKER

Bidemmi lives on the floor above me. We visit back and forth a lot. Bidemmi loves to draw, so when she opens the door I'm often standing there with a marker of some kind or color she doesn't have yet.

She always tries a new marker right away.
First she makes a dot on the paper. Then she
draws a line out from that dot. As she draws,
she tells the story of what she is drawing.
She always starts with the word THIS.
THIS is the door to the subway...

THIS is the door to the subway and THIS is a man leaning on the door. I hope he doesn't fall out when the door opens all of a sudden. His face is a nice face. But it is also not so nice. He has a fat wrinkle on his forehead. It's like my mother's wrinkle. It's from worrying and worrying, my mother says. And his neck is thick and his arms are thick with very big, strong muscles. His shirt is striped blue and white and his skin is dark brown and in his great big hands he has a small white bag. This man looks so strong I think he could even carry a piano on his head. But he is only carrying this little white bag. I wonder what can be in that little bag.

can just see that man going home to his house and walking up the stairs and opening the door to his living room. His living room has a pretty lamp and he switches it right on. His kids are in the kitchen.

"Dee Dee, Dennis, Duane, Dorrie," he calls. "I got something here for you." Then they come out. One sits on one of his legs and one on the other. One leans right in between. And Dee Dee, she climbs round in back and leans over his shoulder. Then he opens the bag and pulls out a cherry. He puts one cherry in each of their mouths and another and another...really red cherries, too. And there they sit eating the cherries and spitting out the pits, eating cherries and spitting out the pits.

And before you can even ask Bidemmi any questions about that story, such as how come the names of all the man's children begin with D, she has another piece of paper ready and is drawing....

THIS is the train seat. And THIS is a tiny white woman sitting on the train seat. She is almost as short as I am, but she is a grandmother. On her head is a black hat with a pink flower, like a rose flower. It has shiny green leaves, like the leaves in my uncle's florist shop. On her feet are old, old shoes. These are the buckles. And in her lap is a big black pocketbook. And in the pocketbook is a bag.

Y̸ou can't really see the bag. But I'll draw it anyway so you can be

sure it's there. It's a little brown paper bag all twisted up tight.

When this woman gets off the train, I know just where she's going.

She's going to hold tight onto the banister and go up the stairs. She's going to hold onto the wall as she walks along the street. And the door to her house is going to be right next to the shoemaker's store. She really likes to hear the shoemaker's machine going round and round and his hammer going tap tap. She waves to him when she goes by his window. Then she climbs up the stairs and opens her door.

There's just one room. It has everything she needs. This is the sink and here's the geranium plant on the window. And on the swing over the plant is her parrot. The parrot is so excited to hear her coming in the house. He is calling, "Little lady, little lady." The parrot is red and yellow and green. It's blue, too.

"I brought something for you," the little woman tells the parrot. She untwists that little brown bag all twisted up tight. She holds it out to the parrot. The parrot takes out a cherry. It's the kind that is light red and sour. The parrot eats it right up.

"You like it?" asks the lady. "You like cherries, honeybird?" She laughs and dumps all of the cherries onto the geranium plant in front of the parrot. "There's your own little cherry tree," she says to the parrot. She stands next to the geranium in her stocking feet, eating cherries with the parrot. The parrot is careful to spit out the pits. They are both eating cherries and spitting out the pits, eating cherries and spitting out the pits.

want to ask Bidemmi some questions, such as if she is sure
the parrot spit out the pits. But she is already remembering
a certain shoelace and a shoe....

THIS is a shoelace. And THIS is a running shoe. It's going to
be purple and white. And here's the other one to match. This is
going to be a boy. These are his long, long legs. This boy looks
a lot like my brother. He's holding onto the straps in the subway.
The train is making him rock back and forth. He's reading the
signs. My brother loves to read. And this boy is tall like my
brother. And he has glasses like my brother. And the same kind of
cap. And the same green and black jacket, too. It has the orange
letters from his team. And when he smiles you can see the
space between his big front teeth like my brother's. In his
pocket is a present.

When he gets off the train at his station, he just runs right up the escalator. He runs right along the streets, jumping on and off the stoops to his house. Before he even gets up the stairs, and he can take them in just two steps, he's hollering to his little sister. "Hey, come on out here. See what I got for you."

And before she can even look out the window
he'll be right in the room in front of her. He'll make
her choose which hand. And there'll be a cherry
in that closed up hand. And it will be the big kind,
such a dark red it's almost black. His little sister
will grab it and eat it up while he yells, "Don't
forget to spit out the pit."

"Is that a story about you?" I ask.

"No," she says. "But this one is going to be about me."

And she draws herself in her favorite beret.

THIS is me. And THIS is my station. I have to walk up the stairs one at a time so the bright sun that is out here in the sky won't make my eyes hurt. But right here on the street, what do you think there is going to be? A man is selling cherries from the back of his truck. His whole truck is going to be cherries. Nothing but cherries. Now see this little purse? I have a little purse in my pocket with some money Mama gave me.

When I show it to the man, he puts a bag on the scale and puts in some cherries. But then he goes ahead and fills it right up to the top and gives it to me.

"Don't eat them up too fast," he tells me.

Now what does that man think? I wasn't going to eat them up fast because I had an important plan. I walk home eating the cherries one by one and saving the pits, eating a cherry and saving the pit. I put every one of the pits in my pocket.

When I get to my street I take them all out. I kneel right down and I poke one in the ground on the edge of our yard. Our yard is a junky old yard. It has this stump where there used to be a tree. But that tree died and they came and cut it down and took it away. Then I poke pits in the ground all over the place. I know if I plant enough of them at least one will grow. I pat the ground smooth. I pour some water on each pit. And I tell those pits to grow… grow and grow.

"Now you want to see how they grow?" Bidemmi asks me. But she doesn't wait for an answer. She is busy laying out all her newest markers. The green, the pink, the red, the purple, the brown, the black, and all the others. She piles up all the papers from the other stories and places a clean sheet on the top. "Now watch," she says.

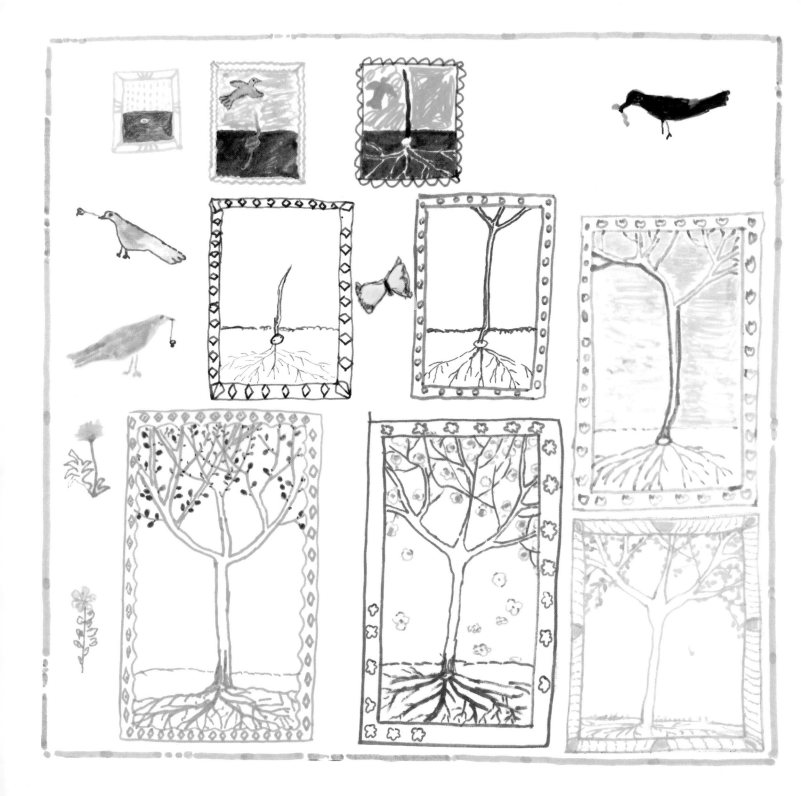

THIS is the pit right here in the middle. And THIS is how it grows. First it makes a little sprout that grows up. Then it makes a little root that grows down. Then that root grows more roots till the ground is full of roots down to here. The sprout grows up to be a little trunk. Branches grow out from the trunk. And from those branches littler branches grow up into the part that is sky. The branches have dark pink buds on them. The buds open up to be light pink flowers. Then come light green leaves. But it seems like there are never going to be any cherries. Everyone is always asking, "Bidemmi, when in the world are those cherries ever going to be ready to eat?"

nd all the time, cherries will be growing right under these leaves, so tiny and green no one even notices them. But I work hard. I come out every single day to chase away the blue jays that are trying to steal the cherries. I chase away the dogs that try to use the yard for their business and the kids who try to carve initials on the tree.

Then one day I come out and the cherries are ripe.
There are so many cherries, the branches reach
right down to the ground. There are red cherries
and dark red cherries and cherries such a deep
red they are almost black.

Then the people come out the back door and the front
door and down the steps. There are enough cherries for
every single one of them. And even for their friends
from Nairobi and Brooklyn, Toronto and St. Paul,
who come down in these airplanes.
So here we all are standing in front of the
airplanes, eating cherries and spitting
out pits, eating cherries and spitting
out pits till we all fall down from
eating so many cherries
and spitting out pits.
And . . .

THIS cherry pit and THIS cherry pit and all the cherry pits start to grow until there is a whole forest of cherry trees right on our block.